The
CURSE of the
WENDIGO

AN AGATE AND BUCK ADVENTURE

by Scott R. Welvaert
illustrated by Brann Garvey

Librarian Reviewer
Marci Peschke
Librarian, Dallas Independent School District
MA Education Reading Specialist, Stephen F. Austin State University
Learning Resources Endorsement, Texas Women's University

Reading Consultant
Mark DeYoung
Classroom Teacher, Edina Public Schools, MN
BA in Elementary Education, Central College
MS in Curriculum & Instruction, University of MN

STONE ARCH BOOKS
Minneapolis San Diego

Vortex Books are published by Stone Arch Books
151 Good Counsel Drive, P.O. Box 669
Mankato, Minnesota 56002
www.stonearchbooks.com

Library of Congress Cataloging-in-Publication Data
Welvaert, Scott R.
    The Curse of the Wendigo: An Agate and Buck Adventure / by
Scott R. Welvaert; illustrated by Brann Garvey.
    p. cm. — (Vortex Books)
    Summary: in 1898, Buck and Agate go into the Canadian
wilderness searching for their missing parents and find themselves in
the middle of a life-and-death battle with the shape-shifting Wendigo
and the even more evil Coyote.
    ISBN-13: 978-1-59889-066-2 (library binding)
    ISBN-10: 1-59889-066-2 (library binding)
    ISBN-13: 978-1-59889-281-9 (paperback)
    ISBN-10: 1-59889-282-7 (paperback)
    [1. Supernatural—Fiction. 2. Brothers and sisters—Fiction.
3. Canada—History—1867–1914—Fiction.] I. Garvey, Brann, ill.
II. Title. III. Series.
PZ7.W46888Cu 2007
[Fic]—dc22   2006007684

Art Director: Heather Kindseth
Graphic Designer: Kay Fraser

Photo Credits
BrandXtrees, cover (back cover and front cover (bottom trees))
Comstock, cover (front cover (top))
Karon Dubke, cover (map and paper)

1 2 3 4 5 6 11 10 09 08 07 06

Printed in the United States of America

TABLE OF CONTENTS

A VOICE IN THE WIND

Buck McGregor had been a light sleeper for all of his sixteen years. His father said it ran in the family. It didn't matter if it was a mouse chewing on a grain of rice in the corner, or a moth flitting around the lantern. Buck was always stirred from his sleep. So when he heard the faint voice calling that cold autumn morning of 1898, he woke up.

"Help . . . help me . . ."

Buck sat up. Moonlight spread across the floor, over a pair of boots, up a pair of legs, and all the way up to his father's face. Even in the grim moonlight, Buck saw his father wink at him.

"Not bad, son. I didn't think you'd hear that," said Roy McGregor.

He was a sturdy man with lanky arms and legs. His trim beard was graying around the edges. His round spectacles caught the moonlight at every turn of his head. Roy was already dressed in his hunting gear.

Buck scratched his head. "Someday I'll be as quick as you."

At the far corner of the cabin, the dull glow from an overhead lantern shined on Buck's mother, Annalisa. Behind her was the wood stove. His father's Mountie uniform hung behind it, ready for duty.

"Roy, let the boy sleep," she said.

Annalisa was a thin woman. She usually kept her hair in a bun nestled behind her head, but that morning it was pulled into a ponytail.

She wore brown pants with a white cotton shirt and a dark brown hunting jacket.

Buck's younger sister, Agate, stirred in her bunk close to the cabin's roof. "Could we cut the light? Some people are trying to sleep," she said.

Annalisa walked across the cabin and stepped up to Agate's bunk. "Sweetheart, go back to sleep."

"That was the idea," Agate said, curling into her blankets.

Against one wall rested an old trunk. Roy lifted its lid and carefully removed a beaded necklace from his neck. He placed it next to a small journal.

"Buck, your mother and I have to check something out," Roy said.

Buck curled up his knees. "It's the voice outside, isn't it?"

Roy reached into the trunk and removed a gun. He quickly slid it into the leather holster on his belt. "Someone sounds very lost, and might need our help."

"That kind of help?" asked Buck as he looked at his father's gun.

Roy looked at his son. "You know I always manage to find a better way. Still, there's no telling what we could run across out there." Roy squatted down next to Buck. "Do you remember that mountain lion we ran across the day we caught all those trout?"

Buck sure did. He remembered his father pulling him into the brush when he heard a growl behind them. Roy had reached for his gun, but he paused and said, "There is always a better way. Around the bend is a clearing. Run!"

Buck sprinted up the hill and around the bend to a ledge over the river valley.

"Get close to the edge!" Roy yelled as he ran. Buck did exactly as his father said, and just as Roy stopped next to him, the big cat sprang from the brush.

The creature swayed its head back and forth and let out a yell Buck thought would stop his heart.

"You can tell when a mountain cat is ready to pounce," whispered Roy. "It'll waggle its butt a little bit right before it leaps. Once it's in the air it can't stop. So right when that cat leaps, dive away to the side."

"But —," Buck said.

"Trust me," said Roy.

The cat paced in front of them, almost as if it was deciding who would be the best to eat first.

"Wait for it," Roy whispered.

The cat hunkered down toward the ground.

"Almost," Roy said.

The mountain lion wagged its backside.

Almost, thought Buck.

The cat jumped with a growl. Without thinking, Buck crouched, then he leaped like a deer and rolled to the side. The mountain lion passed over him and over the edge of the bluff. Buck scrambled on his belly to the edge and looked down. The cat lay thirty feet below on a jumble of large rocks.

"Is he dead?" Buck asked.

Roy crawled over to Buck and looked down to see the cat hobble up onto its feet. "Naw. But that broken leg will make him think twice about attacking a human again."

"You know, Edward," said Roy. "Today is the day you earned your real name. You moved swift and strong back there."

"You became the mighty buck in your actions," said Roy. "Now let your actions become your name: Buck."

WAITING

Now Buck's parents were fully dressed and ready to go into the night. His mother stood at the door. "We won't be long," she said.

"Watch after your sister until we get back," his father said.

Then they were gone. The hanging lantern swung in the breeze from the closing door. Buck watched through the window. As his parents rode deeper into the woods, their own lantern grew smaller and smaller.

His parents often went out to help people. The forests and hills of Canada were vast and not completely mapped, and travelers sometimes became lost.

This time, Buck was worried.

Even though Agate was quiet in her bunk, she was not asleep. Like her brother, she too felt a sense of dread.

Her mind raced. Agate at age ten was smarter than the crack of a whip. Her bed, close to the ceiling, had a secret bookshelf that no one else could see from the floor of the cabin. This was where she kept books on almost every subject — mathematics, poetry, history, biology, and others. But those books seemed useless and far away right now.

Agate rolled over and watched her brother sitting at the window.

She remembered back when she was eight and her father took Buck hunting.

She was jealous because she had wanted to go too. Her mother took her berry picking in the woods instead.

"Berry picking is for babies," Agate had said to herself.

Later that day, they were filling their baskets with plump chokecherries when Annalisa stepped into an old rabbit hole. She screamed in pain. "Elizabeth!" she shouted.

Agate ran to her mother and looked at the broken leg. "That's close to a compound fracture. It almost broke the skin."

Agate grabbed her mother's lower leg and said, "This will hurt a little bit, but I have to set it." The girl tugged hard on the leg. Annalisa screamed again. But in a flash, the leg was no longer misshapen. "I need your hatchet, Mama," said Agate.

Agate scavenged the woods for two strong, straight branches. She laid them next to her mother's broken leg and began ripping her own dress into a long bandage.

She wrapped the strip of cloth tightly around the branches and her mother's leg, forming a sturdy splint. Then she went back into the woods and came out with two long, straight branches. Each one had a Y-shaped crook at the end.

She laid them by her mother's side and measured them from her feet to her armpits.

"You're making crutches?" her mother asked.

"I can't very well carry you out of the woods myself, Mama. I'm only eight."

After a slow journey home, her mother was able to rest in her bed until Roy fetched the town doctor. From that day forward, everyone knew Agate was special.

A week after their rabbit hole adventure, Roy brought home a special gift.

It was a simple leather loop that held a polished Lake Superior agate.

"It appears there are more layers to you than anyone could imagine," said Roy.

"Your clear sharp thinking is like the glassy layers of this agate. Your actions have shown this, so let your actions become your name: Agate."

Roy placed the necklace over his daughter's head. Agate fingered the small stone. It was warm and smooth in her hands.

* * *

Up in her bunk, Agate rubbed her stone. She often did so when she was sad or worried. It seemed to help. "You might as well come down," Buck said. "You aren't asleep."

Outside, the darkness of the woods was overwhelming. It reminded Agate of a giant black beast swallowing up their parents.

Buck turned to her and asked, "Do you feel that?"

"Feel what?" Agate said.

"Like we'll never see them again?"

Agate punched Buck in the shoulder. "Don't say that!"

"Ouch!" Buck rubbed his shoulder. "You're getting stronger."

A dark wind shook the cabin. From deep in the woods a shrill call erupted, like the cry of an eagle and a boar and a wolf all rolled into one. It echoed from tree to tree and valley to valley, until it slowly died away.

For the first time in their young lives, Buck and Agate felt afraid and alone.

CHAPTER 3

"WHERE'D THEY GO?"

Neither Buck nor Agate slept all night. When the sun peeked over the horizon, Buck walked to his father's chest.

"What are you doing?" asked Agate.

He knelt down and held the lock in his hand. "Something's not right," he said. "I'm hoping there might be something in this trunk that gives us a clue."

Buck walked quickly outside and came back a moment later with a large ax.

But before he could swing it down onto the chest, Agate stopped him. "Wait," she said. "There may be a better way."

She reached in her hair and took out two bobby pins. Then she stuck them into the padlock and began to pick the lock.

Buck looked surprised. "When did you learn that?" he asked.

"What do you think I do all day while you guys are hunting?" she said.

After a few moments, the lock sprung open, and they looked inside.

On top were several small journals. There was also a flint and steel to make fire, two pocket knives, a harmonica, an old pistol, their father's beaded necklace, a pouch full of polished stones with strange markings on them, a large feather quill, a broken pair of glasses, and an old hatchet.

Buck looked sad. "I figured Dad kept important stuff in here. I thought we'd find something that could help us."

Agate opened one of the journals and a piece of folded paper fell out.

It was a detailed map of the Canadian woods. It had strange writing and pictures, but it also showed paths and trails they could follow. Agate said, "Maybe this map will help."

"There's only one way to find out," said Buck.

* * *

They quickly prepared for their journey. Agate grabbed a few history books, a trail guide, and a book of old stories. Next she put bread and dried beef into a pack.

Buck led two horses to the front of the cabin. Agate walked to her golden horse and stroked its neck. "Good morning, Sunbeam," she said. She packed her books in the saddlebags and mounted the horse.

She looked over at the white horse and said, "Did Buck give you something to eat, Moonshine?" The horse flicked its tail.

Buck went into the cabin and came out carrying his hunting rifle. He secured it on Moonshine's saddlebag. As he turned around and looked at the cabin, he wondered if his parents would see it again.

"What's wrong, Buck?" Agate asked.

Buck shook his head and mounted Moonshine. "Nothing," he said.

Agate took out her necklace and rubbed the smooth stone. "We'll find them," she said.

As they rode through the forest where Buck had seen their lantern fade away, he felt a strange fear.

He couldn't stop the feeling, so he buried it deep inside him.

They traveled for three hours until they were high atop Blackfoot Ridge. When the wind blew, the forest below them looked like the fur of a great black bear.

"I think I found a clue," said Agate.

"What?" asked Buck.

Agate looked closely at the old map from the journal. "Fiddle. I think it's a town. It's capitalized on the map," she said.

"I don't remember that town. Pa never spoke about it," said Buck.

"Well, it's on the darn map," said Agate. "I bet this ridge here on the map is Blackfoot Ridge. Fiddle is about four knuckles to the northeast. That's about eight miles."

"We'll have to camp overnight, and then we can make it in the morning," said Buck. "We can reach Turtle Creek before nightfall."

When Buck and Agate reached the creek, they tied off the horses in a patch of clover. Agate gathered wood while Buck hunted. He returned with a few quail and they roasted them over a small campfire for dinner.

A while later, Agate was fast asleep in her blanket and Buck sat by the fire nibbling the last pieces of roasted quail. The surrounding forest was dark. The trees overhead rattled their branches in the breeze. Buck wondered who lived in Fiddle. Or was Fiddle a person? Was he a friend? Was he an enemy? Buck shook his head at the thought.

Just then an icy wind blew past Buck. He cocked his ear to a sound. It was a whisper on the wind and it sounded familiar.

"Where'd they go . . . ?"

It was the same sound the wind made the night his parents disappeared.

"Where'd they go . . . ?"

As suddenly as it came, the icy wind died away, and Buck felt the fire's warmth again. Buck grabbed his blanket and huddled next to his sister.

CLAWS IN THE SAND

When Agate woke up, the morning was cool and crisp. She cracked her knuckles, then stood up and stretched her arms and legs. She walked down to the shore of the creek.

Buck was sitting by the edge of the water, his legs crossed, staring at the babbling creek. Agate could always tell when he was worried. Buck would curl the hair above his forehead with his pointer finger. Sometimes Buck curled the hair around his finger so tight it made a knot. As Agate walked up behind him, she saw him pulling his hair.

"Good morning," Buck said without looking at her.

"Blast!" said Agate as sat down next to her brother. "One of these times I'm actually going to sneak up on you."

"Maybe," Buck said.

Agate threw a rock into the creek. Splunk! "What's our plan, Buck?" she asked.

Buck stared up at the sky. "Well, we have to figure out who or what Fiddle is," he said. "After that, I just don't know."

Buck had stopped curling his hair. When he was making plans, Buck didn't have time to worry. "I'll pack up," Agate said.

As soon as his sister left, Buck stood up to walk back to the camp. As he stepped away from the creek, he noticed a set of tracks in the sand.

They looked like a man's, but there were claw markings instead of toes, like bear tracks. But bear tracks weren't this long.

Buck tracked the prints in the sand. They paced up and down the shore and then stopped, right at their campsite! Buck stood up in terror. Whatever it was, it had stood over them while they slept.

Buck took a deep breath and told himself not to be afraid, to be strong, and to protect his sister. "Everything ready to go?" he asked.

Agate stomped on the last few smoking embers and nodded. Together, they mounted their horses and rode off.

All morning they traveled through the forest, heading toward the place marked Fiddle on the map. They rode out of the ravine from Turtle Creek, over Dutchman's Hill, and into Jack Pine Valley. They stopped to refill their canteens at a small brook. Agate got down from her horse and sat on a nearby log. She opened one of their parents' journals and read through it.

"I don't think we know our parents as well as we thought," said Agate.

"What makes you say that?" Buck asked.

Agate flipped through the journal. "These pages. They're filled with all kinds of odd things: maps, diagrams, pictures of weird animals I've never seen before," she said.

Weird animals? Buck thought about the tracks he saw at last night's campsite. He stepped closer to Agate and looked at the open page. In his mother's handwriting was a note that read " . . . and each ash turned into a mosquito . . ." Above the note was a sketch of a large man with fangs.

"What do you think this stuff is, Aggie?"

Agate pointed to the fanged creature. "This drawing comes from an old Tlinget legend," she said. "But in the story the creature was destroyed."

"Destroyed?" asked Buck.

Agate was in deep thought. "I think our parents were involved in something," she said. "Something strange. These journals are filled with weird stuff. There's a river serpent in Minnesota, a railroad ghost in Saskatchewan, and a half-man, half-coyote person all over the place."

Buck knew it was time to tell Agate about the tracks. They could have been made by the creature mentioned in the journal.

"Aggie, um, last night . . ." Buck said.

Before he could finish, they heard a deep voice. "Who trespasses in my woods?"

FIDDLER

A man stood behind them. He was dressed head to toe in buckskin. His graying hair was long and greasy and so was his beard. His eyes were set deep in his skull and burned like two coals on fire. In his hand was a large revolver. It was pointed at Buck and Agate.

Agate ducked behind the log she was sitting on.

Buck waved his hands at the man. "Don't shoot! We're just passing through."

The man stepped closer to them. "Where are you headed?"

"We're looking for Fiddle," said Buck.

The man looked at them strangely. "What for?" he asked.

Agate peeked out from behind the log. "Our parents were helping lost travelers and they disappeared."

The man put away his gun and bent over in laughter. Then he stood back up and looked at Agate. "Lost travelers? Is that what you think? Your parents lied to you."

"They would never lie to us," said Buck.

The man's eyes seemed to be full of fire. "You two are pretty smart, I'll give you that," he said.

He stepped closer to the kids and shook their hands. "My name is Jack Fiddler. You must be Roy and Annalisa's kids. I've known them all my life, but I haven't seen you two since you were little squirts. Come with me. I'll fix you some rabbit stew."

Buck and Agate followed Fiddler back to his wigwam.

The wigwam was a tentlike building made of long, arching poles. Animal skins covered the poles and kept out the wind.

They sat around a large fire pit dug in the dirt floor. Above the fire hung an iron pot simmering with stew. Fiddler handed them each a wooden bowl of stew and a wide wooden spoon.

Agate took a spoonful of stew.

"If Ma and Pa weren't helping lost travelers, what did they go into the woods for?" she asked.

Fiddler looked at her. "To find an ancient spirit that has been around a long, long time. Some think it's a curse, while others think it's power. Tribes have a name for it: Wendigo."

"What's a Wendigo?" Buck asked.

Agate said, "It's a curse on anyone who eats the flesh of another human. Tribes told the story of the Wendigo to stop people from becoming cannibals during harsh winters."

"You know about this?" Buck asked.

"I read a lot," said Agate. "The curse turns a person into a half-human, half-animal creature called the Wendigo. It's just a story."

Buck swallowed hard. "I think it might be more than just a story," he said.

Fiddler moved closer to Buck. "Have you seen the Wendigo?" he asked.

Buck looked at his sister and Fiddler. "I think I've seen its tracks, with claws at the toes like a bear, or a wolf," Buck said.

Fiddler leaned forward wringing his hands. He was excited. "Yes! That is the track of the Wendigo," Fiddler said.

"What does this thing have to do with our parents?" said Agate.

Fiddler sat back down, across from the fire. "Your parents and I are members of an ancient order," he said. "We have sworn to fight evil in all its forms. The Wendigo is just one of many spirits we hunt."

"But Ma and Pa went looking for lost travelers," said Buck. "I heard the voice."

"Did you?" asked Fiddler. "What did it say? 'Help . . . help me . . .'" An icy chill ran up and down Buck's spine.

"What you heard, boy, were the cries of the creature's victims," said Fiddler. "Most people cannot hear what you heard. Only those with the blood of the Majictaw in their veins can. Certainly two purebloods like you would have heard it."

"What did you call us?" asked Buck.

Fiddler chuckled. "Your parents hid their past well. In the history of the world, there have only been a handful of purebloods born. And every single one of them attained greatness. All except one, but that is a story for another time. You two are purebloods because both of your parents are Majictaw."

"I've never heard of Majictaw before," said Agate. "Is that a tribe from Canada?"

Fiddler shook his head. "They are from everywhere. But, Majictaw do not reveal themselves until they are called."

"How were you called?" asked Agate.

"A call can come in a dream. For some it is just a feeling. The call pulls that person. You may not even know you have been called until you are standing in front of the elders and getting your orders."

"Blazes!" Buck exclaimed.

"Sometimes I go to bed at night and when I awake I'm in a different place," Fiddler said.

He paused. "You know, I might help you two out a little more. Where is that map I saw you looking at earlier?"

Agate took the map from her pocket and handed it to Fiddler.

"Your parents did mark off my location," said Fiddler, "as well as the location of the ancient Majictaw burial grounds to the north. It is forbidden to reveal these things. If this map were to get into the wrong hands, it would be disastrous."

Buck grabbed the map back. "Then we'll make sure we hang on to it."

Fiddler stared at Buck. "We need to go to the burial grounds. This map is your call. Your parents are calling for you."

Buck and Agate looked at each other.

Agate rubbed the stone on her necklace. There was a strange energy between her and Buck that she had never felt before.

It felt like an invisible hand was moving them. She was sure Buck felt it too.

Buck said, "At first light we'll leave for the burial grounds."

* * *

Buck woke up in the middle of the night, just as Fiddler was sneaking out of the dark wigwam. Buck quickly followed him up a hill, but when he reached the top, Fiddler was gone.

Then, although it was still early fall, it began to snow.

Buck held out his hand and caught a few flakes on his hand. He watched them quickly melt away.

Suddenly, the hair on the back of Buck's neck stood up. Across the valley, something crunched through the trees.

Then came another massive footstep. The snow fell faster. Another footstep. It was getting closer.

Buck sat with his back against a tree and pulled out his hunting knife.

Something crunched behind his tree. The branches rustled overhead. Buck heard it sniffing the air.

Buck turned his head to see a steam of vapor drifting from behind the tree.

Then, suddenly, it screamed. A giant shadow leaped away, breaking branches in its path. As the sound grew faint, Buck stood up and took a deep breath.

Fiddler jumped out from behind the tree.

"Did you see it?" Fiddler asked.

Buck put his knife back in its sheath. "I didn't see it."

Fiddler's face was red with excitement. His eyes were shining in the moonlight. "There's a Wendigo in the woods," he said with a crazy grin. "It's time to go hunting, my friend!"

CHAPTER 6

COYOTE

"Blackberry Brook is just over the next pass," said Fiddler.

He, Buck, and Agate had been through wooded hills all morning. The afternoon sun blazed in the cool, autumn sky.

"Fiddler, why don't you go on ahead and find us a nice spot for lunch," said Buck.

"Will do," said Fiddler. Then he slapped his reins and his horse took off down the trail.

Buck watched him ride away and then waited for Agate to catch up.

"How far are we, Aggie?" he asked.

"We probably have two more days of riding before we reach the burial grounds," Agate said. She folded up the map and placed it in her pocket. She noticed Buck was looping his hair around his finger again.

"Something has you spooked," Agate said. "Are you still thinking about that Wendigo?"

"I think it's following us," said Buck.

"What would it want from us?" asked Agate.

"From the sound of it huffing and sniffing behind that tree last night, I'd say it wants us for dinner!"

"But it ran away," Agate said.

"I think Fiddler scared it off."

Agate looked as if she was trying to solve a puzzle. "Was it horrible looking?"

"I didn't see it. But I felt it. Its head rattled the tree branches. It had this awful scream."

"Halloo! I've found us a nice spot here!" Fiddler was waving and squatting at the banks of a small creek at the bottom of a hill.

As they trotted down the hill, Agate took out the map again and looked at the markings.

She rubbed her fingers over the simple sketch of the burial grounds.

"The map!" Agate said. "The Wendigo is after the map. Remember what Fiddler said? He said that the map could be used to find the elders."

"But this thing is just a dumb animal," Buck said. "It hunts and eats. It can't read."

Agate took one of her books out of a saddlebag and read out loud.

"The Wendigo spirit is known to take over the body of the cursed. This happens once the person eats the flesh of another human being." She took a breath, then went on.

"The cursed are often isolated from society and forced to live in exile. Wendigos are also known to control the weather. They take on the appearance of their surroundings, often choosing forms such as bears, wolves, deer, elk, coyotes, or foxes. There is no known cure, magic, or amulet to reverse the curse of the Wendigo. Only death can release the curse."

"So this thing is a person?" asked Buck.

Agate clapped her book shut. "Yes."

"Impossible," said Buck.

Buck and Agate rode down to the brook. They tied up their horses and drank from the bubbling waters.

Agate wiped her mouth and said, "So how many Wendigos have you killed, Mr. Fiddler?"

Fiddler sat back on his haunches. "About two dozen over my lifetime," he said, carefully.

"I save a bone from each one," he added.

"How can you tell when someone is a Wendigo?" asked Agate.

"You can always tell. A person's eyes go black when the Wendigo is in them. Their eyes grow as black as the heart of Coyote."

"Who is Coyote?" asked Buck.

"Coyote is the father of all evil," said Fiddler. "He has a hand in all doom across the world. Some say he has walked the earth from the beginning of time. His spirit jumps from man to man. When his body withers and dies, his spirit moves to a new body."

Agate stood up at the edge of the brook and asked, "Have you ever seen Coyote?"

Fiddler shook his head. "No, but your father did once."

Fiddler took a deep breath and continued.

"He tracked him to a great temple, deep in the South American jungles. He said Coyote was so old, his nose was sunken in and his skin was brown and wrinkled. He was nothing but a skeleton."

Agate moved closer to Fiddler and sat on her knees. "What happened?"

Fiddler looked into the distance as he spoke.

"Your father snuck into Coyote's chamber, and drew the great Halynn'Pano with the intent to kill."

Buck asked, "What is Halynn'Pano?"

"It is an ancient sword passed down through the generations of Elders. It carries many Majictaw spells. Armed with that, your father thought he could finally rid the world of evil. As he drew the sword, Coyote used all his dark powers to paralyze him."

"Your father said that if you stared into the blackness of his eyes too long, you would never return. Coyote stood over him, whispered something into his ear, and then left. It was three days before Coyote's powers released him."

Agate looked at Fiddler, amazed. "What did Coyote say to Papa?"

Fiddler shook his head and replied, "Your father never said."

Buck and Agate could not believe their ears. Their father was not just a father. He was not just a Mountie.

He was a powerful warrior.

A spirit hunter.

"What about Mama?" Agate asked. "What part does she play in all this?"

Fiddler stood up and walked toward the three horses.

"We need to get moving if we want to cross Kodiak River before sunset," he said.

Buck said, "The Kodiak is miles away."

Fiddler squinted up at the sun and then said, "Then we have to move quickly. It is only a few hours before nightfall."

ATTACK
AT THE RIVER

They arrived at a ravine along the raging Brown Bear River after three hours of hard riding. The river roared with water from the wet summer and would be difficult to cross.

Fiddler's eyes were dark and his smile was wide. "My friends, the hunt has come full circle! Can you feel the blood race in your veins?" He leaped off his horse, reached into his jacket, and pulled out a long hunting knife.

"You must cross the river now!" he said. "Once across, ride hard and don't look back! This hunt is not yours. It is mine. Now go! Find your parents!"

Fiddler howled to the rising moon and ran screaming into the forest.

"Let's go!" Buck yelled to Agate.

They spurred their horses into the deep water. Agate felt Sunbeam's muscles beneath her tightening up with each stride. Soon, the horses were nearly submerged.

A cry raged from the woods behind them. Buck recognized the call of the Wendigo.

Agate turned her head but Buck yelled, "Don't look back!"

They galloped on and heard another howl. The Wendigo grew near.

Agate urged her horse toward the far shore. She shielded her eyes as the sun set behind the trees and saw darkness creep through the forest. The sky grew white. Snowflakes began to fall.

"Move!" screamed Buck, and he slapped Sunbeam's rump. She lurched forward and ran up the shore. Buck followed on Moonshine. They rode off into the forest.

After hours of riding furiously, Buck and Agate grew cold and strangely tired. Agate felt like she was in a dream. She slipped off her horse and fell to the ground, but she didn't care. She wanted to sleep.

Lying on the ground, Agate saw the forest open up, and out of the trees came the Wendigo. It was tall, with matted, gray fur. It looked like a wolf or a coyote. Dead tree branches sprouted from its skin. It moved closer and closer.

Agate felt its claws brushing against her jacket. Her eyes were too heavy. She barely kept them open. Then she saw a strange man wave a blue light at the Wendigo and it disappeared. She dropped into sleep.

In a dream, Buck saw the Wendigo reach out for Agate. He saw an old man with an ancient face.

A blue light burst from his hands and the creature ran off.

Buck opened his eyes and realized he was not at home.

The roof above him was made of branches. Wool blankets covered him.

He felt hot, so he pushed them aside and sat up. Across the hut in another bed lay Agate, bundled up to her neck in blankets.

Buck quietly grabbed his boots from the floor, put them on, and snuck across the room.

Buck nudged Agate's shoulder, "Aggie, get up," said Buck.

Agate held onto her blankets tightly and said, "It's so warm in here."

"Come on," said Buck. "We need to go."

But before she came fully awake, a tall woman with golden brown skin ducked through the doorway of the cabin and said, "Well, the purebloods live."

Buck walked in front of Agate to shield her. "Who are you?" he asked.

"I am Calandra," said the woman in a voice smooth and sweet as maple syrup.

Agate was fully awake now. She asked, "Are you Majictaw?"

The woman nodded. "I'm a Majictaw warrior, sent by the Council of Elders, to help you find your parents."

"Are you the one who fought the Wendigo?" Buck asked, but he knew the wrinkled face he'd seen in his dream could not be mistaken for the beautiful woman before him.

She laughed. "No, dear one, but you shall meet him soon enough"

"Well, can you tell us," Buck asked, "why is the Wendigo after us?"

"The Wendigo craves human flesh."

Agate pushed Buck from in front of her, "Then why didn't he get us when he had the chance?"

From the nearby forest a loud shriek echoed. It sounded like a wild boar, an eagle, and a wolf all at once.

Suddenly, snowflakes began to fall.

"There will be time for questions, but now you must follow me. Quickly!" Calandra rushed out the door, and Buck and Agate followed.

FLYING

CHAPTER 9

"We must hurry, children. The Wendigo is not far from us now," Calandra said.

"Why do we have to keep running?" asked Buck. "I'm a pretty good shot with a pistol or a rifle."

"It takes more than bullets to stop a Wendigo," said Calandra. "I need to get you to the temple. You'll be safe there."

The forest grew thin with trees, leaving big gaping spaces to ride through. In front of them loomed a hill covered in pine trees.

"We're getting close," said Calandra. "There are spells in this area to keep people away. You would do best to close your eyes."

Buck and Agate closed their eyes tightly. But Agate was too curious. She was amazed at what she saw.

The trees were alive. Their branches turned into long arms and fingers. Their trunks split and became legs. Faces opened up in the bark. They stomped and bounded toward them.

Agate spurred her horse to run faster, but the trees gained on her. Agate felt their branches scrape her back. A little pine tree jumped onto her horse and was trying to bite her arm. Agate looked over at Buck and his eyes were open too. He was fighting off several little trees that had climbed up onto Moonshine.

Suddenly, the trees jumped away from them. Their horses were heading toward the edge of a cliff. Buck and Agate screamed and braced for the fall.

The fall didn't come. They rode through the air. A river rolled far below, like a thin blue ribbon. A hill came into view, and a few moments later the horses' hooves struck ground again.

When Buck and Agate dismounted, Calandra rushed over to them. "I knew you two were powerful," she said, "but I had no idea. It takes all of my energy to hold three horses above the valley. But with you two it was so much easier. You helped."

"But how?" asked Agate. "I don't remember doing anything."

"Sometimes danger can focus your energy," said Calandra. "In time you'll learn to focus it when your mind is at ease."

"Where are we?" asked Buck.

THE HIDDEN TEMPLE

Calandra stepped to the sheer face of the hill and said, "This is a great temple."

Buck looked around and said, "I don't see a temple."

Calandra cleared brush away from the side of the hill, revealing a flat stone surface. A large ring was carved in the wall. Along the ring were thirty notches in the stone. Calandra pulled a cloth pouch from her belt and opened it. She took out five stones, each a different color.

Agate said, "Our Papa had a bag of those stones in his trunk. We brought them with us." Agate reached in her pocket and pulled out Roy's pouch.

"Our rune stones have many purposes," said Calandra. She began placing her five stones in notches along the circle. When the last stone clicked into place, the wall rumbled and slid sideways.

"Go," Calandra said, motioning to the dark passageway. "Follow this until you reach the sanctuary. I must go back."

Calandra closed the door. Buck and Agate followed the passageway. Flaming torches on the walls lit the way.

They came to a large room lit by hundreds of candles. At the far end of the room was a high wall with a carving of the sun at the top and ancient tapestries hung all around.

The tapestries showed symbols for mountains, swamps, and deserts. Others showed prairies, oceans, and forests.

Below the forest tapestry, someone knelt on a mat, facing the wall. Without moving, the figure said, "Are you feeling better?"

He was a very old Asian man wearing a buckskin jacket, the same man from Buck's weird dream.

He was the man with the blue light.

He stood up. "I am glad you have answered my call," he said.

"You're the one who saved us from the Wendigo," said Buck.

"My name is Igam," he said. "I am the head of the Council of Elders. The Majictaw. I'm afraid your parents, young ones, are in grave danger."

"Can you send someone to save them?" pleaded Agate.

Igam turned to look at the tapestry, as if he were reading it. "I have already sent three hunters into the burial grounds to rescue them. The Wendigo has devoured them all."

"I thought the Majictaw were powerful," said Agate.

Igam shook his head.

"We are powerful people, Miss Elizabeth," he said. "But the Wendigo grows stronger as it feeds, especially when it has slain a Majictaw. He has taken the lives of three already. One more would leave it too powerful."

"Then we will go," said Agate. "Someone has to save our parents."

Igam muttered as if he were talking to someone else. "There must be a better way."

Agate stepped closer to him and said, "This is the better way."

"Life is a series of choices," said Igam. "I hope for your sake this is a good one. Follow me. If you go, you will not go alone."

Igam led them to a room that shimmered with silver and gold. Gleaming swords and daggers covered the walls. A velvet box in the corner overflowed with golden and silver rings.

Buck saw only one thing. On the far wall hung a shining silver sword. He remembered the story Fiddler told about his father. "That's the Halynn'Pano," said Buck.

Igam was surprised. "You have heard of the Sword of Shades?" he asked, handing it to Buck.

"In a way," said Buck.

Agate looked anxious. "What do I get?"

Igam laughed. "You do not need anything. You already wear the Pedne Stone around your neck. When used properly, time itself may be slowed down. It will be very useful."

Suddenly, Igam seemed to falter. His face grew pale. "I sense much danger," he said.

"Of course, the Wendigo," said Buck.

Igam looked worried. "Not just Wendigo. I sense someone far more powerful and evil. Since the beginning of life, one force has always tried to destroy the Majictaw. Without us, he rules alone and the whole planet will fall to his power. His only hope to destroy us is to become one of us and take our power from within."

Agate looked puzzled. "Who?" she asked.

Igam took a deep breath. "Coyote."

Coyote was deep within the burial grounds to the north. He limped toward a dungeon cell that was lit by a single torch. Shackled to the wall were Roy and Annalisa McGregor.

Coyote limped over to Annalisa and leaned into her until she smelled his rotting flesh. "It won't be long now, my dear," he said.

"You monster!" yelled Annalisa.

Coyote shuffled over to Roy. "There was a time when you thought I was weak, that you had the power to bring me to an end. I could have crushed your bones to powder, but I didn't. I let you live. Today you will return the favor and give me life."

Roy spit in Coyote's face. "You are weak, Coyote. Without a new body, you will waste away."

Coyote reached up with a bony hand and wiped the spit from his dried skull. "I have had millions of bodies, McGregor. Millions! But you are wrong. I am not here to take your body, as much as that would please me. I am here for another. You, my old friend, are merely the bait."

Roy suddenly realized why he and Annalisa were allowed to live. Coyote was after the children. If he took over a pureblood body, he would gain incredible power.

Coyote cocked his head and said, "Look at it this way, your son will rain darkness into the world." Then he limped over to Annalisa and held her chin in his bony hand. "Or perhaps it will be your daughter? How nice of you to give me a choice."

*　*　*

Buck and Agate left the temple on their horses and rode a long time. On his back, Buck wore the Sword of Shades, Halynn'Pano. As he rode through the cold night, he felt the sword's warmth. It vibrated with energy.

Agate held her necklace stone in one hand as she rode. It, too, felt warm to the touch. She looked ahead at her brother. With the silver sword on his back, he looked bigger and older. Then Agate looked down at her necklace. The agate glowed. She held it tight in her hands and closed her eyes. She saw images of a forest covered in snow. Something was wrong. The trees were dead. They reached from the ground like black, bony hands.

Later that afternoon, Agate saw the real trees from her vision. "We must be near the burial grounds," she said.

After a few moments they came to a hilltop clearing. It was covered with large, ancient gravestones, some of them taller than Buck. They tied their horses to a tree and then walked between the gravestones.

Each stone had markings carved in them. Agate reached in her pack, pulled out the small pouch, and laid some rune stones across her palm. The markings on them matched the markings on the gravestones.

"Can you read them?" asked Buck.

Agate looked at the rune stones on her palm, trying to make words out of them. After a few tries she stopped. "Give me a minute," she said. Agate took out the journals. Thousands of markings spread across the pages. She ran her finger over the symbols on the gravestone and then pointed to each one on the page.

"Ar-Ch-Uss-Ah-Mah-Tuss," Agate read off the gravestone. "Th-Pur-Tek-Tur."

Agate ran to another gravestone that towered over her. She read, "Mah-Jus-Ras-Pur-Uh-Toh. Th-Kah-Lek-Tur." Then she retraced the markings with her finger. "The Collector," she said. "The Collector!"

She ran over to the first gravestone and ran her fingers over the markings again. "The Protector!" she said. "These must be the graves of ancient Majictaw warriors. Hey, Buck, I can read this!"

"Over here, Agate! I found something!"

Agate packed up her books and stones, and followed her brother's voice. He knelt on the ground.

"These are the same tracks from our campsite," Buck said.

Agate looked around and said, "The Wendigo is here."

"I'd say these tracks are about twelve hours old," said Buck.

"Where do they come from?" asked Agate.

Buck pointed to the entrance of an underground tunnel. "It's been in and out of that tunnel every day," said Buck. "Ever since Ma and Pa disappeared."

Agate said, "That means —"

"There's a good chance they're down there too," said Buck.

Agate swallowed hard and followed her big brother to the tunnel. It was a tall opening surrounded by a stone archway. On the stones were the same markings as on the gravestones.

"I can read this," said Agate.

She held the journal in one hand and pointed to the markings on the archway.

"I think it reads, 'Strength lies beneath these stones.'"

Suddenly, a cold wind blew.

Buck reached back and grabbed his sword. It felt heavy. He felt the spirit of each great warrior who had held it before him. Their energy entered his hands. It flowed through him until it reached his heart and mind. As he shifted the blade back and forth, he saw the reflections of the past warriors.

Buck and Agate looked at each other and stepped into the darkness of the tunnel.

CHAPTER 12

AN OLD FRIEND

Symbols covered the walls of the tunnel.

"What do they say?" asked Buck

"They're warnings," said Agate. "Ancient cultures always leave warnings to keep looters from raiding their tombs. But there are so many tunnels! How will we know which one leads to Papa and Mama?"

Buck said, "Leave that to me."

He ripped one of the torches from the wall and squatted down to see the footprints on the dusty floor.

Buck and Agate walked down the tunnel holding the torch closely to the floor.

They followed the footprints through countless corridors. Soon their trail ran across another set of tracks, then another, and another. Before long, they couldn't remember which way they had been.

Agate looked around and said, "There's got to be a better way." She held tight to the stone on her necklace. It became warm in her hand and Agate closed her eyes. Without opening them, she said, "This way," and began to walk.

Buck followed his sister for almost half an hour before she opened her eyes in front of a dim cell. Two figures were chained to the wall. "Mama! Papa!" Agate cried.

Buck ran up to his mother and said, "Don't worry. We'll get you out."

Agate ran over to her father and hugged and kissed him. "Papa!" she said.

Roy McGregor looked down at his daughter and smiled a tired but proud smile.

"Let me get you out of these chains," Agate said. She took out a hairpin and shoved it in the lock. She stuck her tongue out as she concentrated. After a moment the lock clicked open and she began working on the other lock.

Buck lifted his sword into the air and was about to swing it down on the chains that held his mother. Roy stepped behind him and stopped him. "There is always a better way," he said.

Roy gently took the sword from Buck and looked at it slowly as if it were the most precious thing on earth. "Ah! Halynn'Pano, the Sword of Shades."

Agate stepped in between them and began to pick the locks chaining her mother.

"What's a shade?" asked Buck.

"A shade is a spirit, a soul," said Roy. "This is called the Sword of Shades because it holds the spirit of the user. When you hold this sword you have the power and strength of all those before you. Should you die with that sword in your hand, you too will become part of the sword forever."

Annalisa stepped forward, rubbing her wrists, and said, "We need to get out of here."

A figure stepped out of the shadows.

He was dirty and bloody from head to toe. His clothes were torn to rags, and gashes crisscrossed his face and arms. He looked on the brink of death.

It was Jack Fiddler.

"Friends," he gasped. "I thought we were all done for."

"We thought you were dead," said Agate.

"Not yet," Fiddler said. "It was the only way I could ensure your safety, by staying back and fighting that monster while you two escaped."

Roy stepped forward with the sword and pointed it directly at Fiddler's chest.

"You will go no farther, Fiddler," said Roy.

Agate said, "What are you doing, Papa?"

"He helped us," said Buck.

Roy stepped closer to Fiddler and said, "Only to help himself."

"What are you talking about?" asked Buck.

Annalisa stepped forward and held her hands out to the children.

"Your father's right," she said.

"Fiddler was only trying to get you here," Annalisa went on. "He's not who he seems. He might have been our friend long ago, but he's changed. Fiddler is the Wendigo."

That's when Agate saw it. Fiddler's eyes flashed pure black.

"Did you see that?" she said. "His eyes. He really is the Wendigo!"

Roy grabbed Fiddler by the back of his hair. "Lead us to Coyote, and we will end this once and for all."

Fiddler bent backward and screamed. His voice grew deep and monstrous. "You'll never escape these ruins. He'll get your boy, and I'll get my cure. You've failed!"

Fiddler reared back and swung at Roy. Roy flew across the dungeon. His sword clattered to the floor.

Fiddler screamed in pain again. His body was making strange noises.

Bones cracked and popped. Clothes ripped, buttons snapped. Fiddler ran past them, limping. His face twisted with fangs and fur. His eyes shone black.

In a flash, the Wendigo was gone.

"THIS IS WHERE IT ENDS"

CHAPTER 13

Buck picked up the sword and Annalisa rushed over to the motionless Roy. "Roy!" she screamed. She lifted his head off the floor.

Roy looked around at his family and said, "Get above ground. Coyote is near."

Buck and Annalisa helped Roy to his feet and led him out of the dungeon.

When they emerged from the tunnels, the full moon shined directly overhead. On the damp ground, an eerie fog rolled among the gravestones. Buck looked around. Something wasn't right.

"This is where it must end," Roy said.

Annalisa and Buck eased Roy to his knees. Buck reached into his boot and unsheathed a small silver dagger he had snuck from the weapon room. He handed it to his father.

Roy looked at the dagger, and then at his son. His face had grown pale. "Take your mother and sister and run away."

Tears welled up in Buck's eyes. "There must be a better way, Pa," he said. "There is always a better way."

Roy smiled. "This is the better way, son. Now go. Save your mother and sister."

"Touching," said an eerie voice from behind a gravestone. Coyote limped into the moonlight. "I hate to spoil the family reunion," Coyote said, "but I believe you have something of mine."

"You and I have unfinished business," said Roy, grimly.

"Your family won't get far," said Coyote. "You are deader than I, old friend, and there is no one to save them."

Buck, Agate, and Annalisa ran off to the horses.

"Death is only a beginning, Coyote," said Roy. "If you weren't so frightened by it, you might have learned that."

Coyote lashed a backhand across Roy's face. "To live forever is a gift greater than any human life. And I will take great pleasure in ending yours!"

Coyote reached his hand out for Roy's neck, but Roy avoided him.

Roy grabbed Coyote around the neck, pulled him close, and pressed a golden amulet to his forehead.

Coyote screeched as the amulet burned into his skull.

"This should hold you long enough," said Roy.

Coyote shook in Roy's arms as holes tore through his skin and white light beamed out of them. He grew still and fell to the ground.

Roy dragged himself over to a large gravestone and leaned against it. His head was throbbing and his vision was fading. He looked up to the moonlit sky and knew he was dying. With his last ounce of strength, he hurled the golden amulet over the edge of the hill.

* * *

"We should stop and rest the horses," said Annalisa.

"Pa said to keep running and not look back," said Buck.

"Coyote's powers are swift and strong," said Annalisa. "But we would be dead by now if your father had failed."

Everyone dismounted. Buck tied up the horses. Agate sat on a nearby log. Annalisa sat next to her and gave her a hug.

"But there had to be a better way, Mama," said Aggie. "There is always a better way."

"Sometimes you have to think further into the future, to the greater good," said Annalisa through her own tears. "That's what your father would want us to do now."

Buck threw some sticks on a small fire that crackled and popped. Then he said, "So what was the greater good?"

"Saving you children," said Annalisa. "A child born of two Majictaw is so special that it attracts the ambitious and evil. That is why Coyote wanted you. With the body of a pureblood, he would be unstoppable."

All night, an icy wind blew through the McGregor's camp. The fire bent and flickered.

The wind formed an evil whisper. "Where'd they go . . ."

Annalisa sat up into the wind and looked at Agate's necklace. It was glowing brightly. A fluffy snow began to fall.

"You know they'll be mine!" the wind said.

"Never, Fiddler!" said Annalisa under her breath.

The wind and snow blew fiercely. Annalisa took one long, last look at the sleeping children and then ran off into the thick forest.

With the bright moonlight, Annalisa saw easily in the dark forest. She walked to the center of a clearing. At first, she saw no sign of the Wendigo, but she knew he was close. Then, behind her, something rose up out of the snow.

Annalisa looked down at her hands. They glowed with blue fire.

"You've become old and weak, Lisa."

She turned quickly and pummeled the Wendigo with both hands. Blue fire exploded and sent the beast flying backward into a tree. The impact split the mighty oak in two.

The Wendigo stood up, picked up the broken oak tree, and hurled it at her.

Annalisa jumped, but the Wendigo snatched her up in its mighty claws. She laid her hands on the Wendigo's eyes and its face erupted in blue flames. Dropping her, the Wendigo bent over in great pain. Its screams echoed through the forest.

Annalisa jumped onto the creature's back and raised her fiery hands for one last strike. The Wendigo reached back with its hand and grabbed her ankle. Once it had her, it tossed her through the trees. Annalisa screamed as the blue fire on her hands died away.

The Wendigo came for her and she knew she had one word left to utter.

* * *

"Run!"

Agate snapped awake and cried, "Mama!"

She looked down and saw her necklace glow. Agate kicked Buck in the shin and said, "Buck, we have to go!"

Agate was up packing their things and getting the horses ready.

Buck saw Agate's necklace glowing brightly and he immediately jumped up.

"Where's Ma?" asked Buck.

Agate looked at him with a sad face and Buck knew their mother was gone.

Somehow he knew she had sacrificed herself, just as their father had.

They rode fast and hard through the forest. Near the eastern horizon, Buck saw morning light. He knew they were nearing Cutface Peak. A plan grew in his mind.

They arrived back at the path that led to the temple. Buck stopped.

Agate turned. "What's wrong?"

"I don't want to run anymore," said Buck. "If I can lure him to the top of the peak, I think I can beat him."

"Are you crazy?" asked Agate. "That thing is huge. You won't last three seconds!"

"Is this what you want?" asked Buck. "Running all the time? We need to face it."

"So what did you have in mind?" she asked.

"Follow me," said Buck, and he spurred his horse up the path to Cutface Peak.

The pine trees looked dark and eerie as they rode past them. Halfway up the peak, it began to snow. The stars began to fade as morning bloomed on the horizon.

"It's coming," she said to Buck.

Buck looked behind them and saw the snow blowing up the hillside toward them. He stopped and dismounted. Agate stopped too.

"What are we doing?" she asked.

Buck ran behind a large rock off to the side and said, "Come here."

Agate ran with him and after a few moments they came to a small hideaway cave on the side of the peak. Buck pointed inside and said, "Take Sunbeam and Moonshine and wait in here until I come back."

"You can't beat that thing alone!" said Agate, her eyes ablaze.

"I have the sword," said Buck. "I've held it and felt its power. You heard Pa. The spirits of past warriors rest in that blade. This is their time to wake up and stand for me. I feel it."

Agate saw in Buck's face that he believed.

"Fine," said Agate.

She ran up to him and hugged him harder than she ever had before. She felt tears welling in her eyes and said, "I'll see you when you get back."

"I promise," said Buck, and then he ran out of the cave.

Buck ran through the driving snow to reach the top of Cutface Peak. He walked to the edge and looked down. It was quite a drop. Now all he had to do was wait for the beast to show up. Like they had for the mountain cat when he and his dad had gone fishing, all he had to do was wait.

Buck turned around and the Wendigo was already standing there. He looked into the face of the beast and reached for the sword strapped to his back. The Wendigo swung his mighty paw at him, knocking him to the ground.

Buck stood and drew his sword.

As soon as his fingers touched the hilt, he felt stronger and swifter. His body felt warmer.

The Wendigo spoke in a fiendish whisper.

"She died quietly, boy."

Buck's face grew red and he charged at the beast. He swung the sword hard at the creature. But the Wendigo held out its thick claws and blocked the blade.

Buck continued to swing the sword. The weapon moved easily for him. But with each swing, the Wendigo blocked.

Buck felt his body getting warmer. The sword felt lighter. Buck could predict where each of the beast's swings was coming from. Each time the Wendigo swung, Buck blocked it with the sword.

Then he saw an opening. He spun, and in a single stroke, cut the Wendigo's arm off above its elbow.

Buck smiled and felt good.

But his pause was a mistake. The Wendigo swung its good hand at Buck and struck, knocking the sword out of his hands and into the brush.

Buck stepped back. He was nearing the edge. It was his only way out.

But he needed to take the Wendigo with him.

Suddenly, the Wendigo grabbed Buck by the neck and lifted him off the ground.

"You ruined everything, boy! Coyote was going to cure me! Now I am cursed with this shape forever!"

Suddenly, it stopped.

The beast released him and howled in pain.

When the Wendigo toppled over, Buck saw Agate standing behind it. Her hands glowed with blue fire.

Together, they watched the Wendigo. The Sword of Shades was still stuck in its furry back from where Agate had struck.

The creature began to shrink and shudder. Bones cracked and popped. Smoke poured from the Wendigo's eyes, ears, and mouth. Its fur and fangs fell out. A weak, gurgling sound escaped from the creature as it slumped into the snow.

Buck and Agate walked over to the motionless body. It was indeed Jack Fiddler, their parents' longtime friend.

Agate pulled the sword from Fiddler's back. She handed it to Buck and said, "I believe this is yours."

Buck looked down at the body. "What did he do to deserve a curse like this?" the boy asked.

"In his case, it was starve to death, or eat flesh to survive," Agate said. "His one bad decision led to many others. Before he knew it, Fiddler was so far off his path, so far from good, he didn't know how to get back."

Buck looked at Fiddler again. He felt sorry for him.

"There is always a better way," said Buck.

Agate smiled at her brother and said, "Yes. There always is."

THE WHISPER ON THE WIND
THE TRUTH ABOUT THE WENDIGO

The Wendigo has haunted myths and folktales told by the Algonquin tribes of North America for centuries. The creature's name comes from an old Algonquin word, witiku, which means "evil spirit" or "spirit that devours humans."

According to ancient legends, a Wendigo is a human possessed by an evil spirit. Lonely hunters might encounter the spirit in the vast woods. Others might become possessed during a nightmare. Still others transform into Wendigos if they resort to cannibalism during a famine or when trapped by a blizzard.

The Wendigo, half-human and half-beast, stands fifteen feet tall. It has giant teeth, blazing eyes, and a long, drooling tongue. It can blend in with a forest and become almost invisible.

The Wendigo is stronger and faster than humans. Some stories say it is made of snow and that one way to destroy the monster is to melt its icy heart.

During the early 1900s, a Wendigo was reportedly seen several times around the town of Roseau, Minnesota, near the Canadian border. Each time the creature appeared, an unexpected death followed soon afterward.

In the fall of 1907, an 87-year-old Cree man from Canada named Jack Fiddler pled guilty to the murder of a woman from his tribe. He claimed he had to stop her from transforming into a Wendigo. Fiddler also insisted that, during his lifetime, he had killed fourteen of the creatures. No one has been able to disprove his claim.

⟶ ABOUT THE AUTHOR ⟿

Scott R. Welvaert lives in Chaska, Minnesota, with his wife and two daughters. He has written many children's books. Most recently, he has written about Helen Keller, the Donner Party, and Thomas Edison. Scott enjoys reading and writing poetry and stories. He also enjoys playing video games and watching the Star Wars movies with his children.

⟶ ABOUT THE ILLUSTRATOR ⟿

Brann Garvey grew up in the great state of Iowa, where he studied art and visual communications. He graduated from the Minneapolis College of Art and Design with a degree in illustration. Brann is usually found with one or more of the following: a pencil in his hand, a comic book, a remote for watching DVDs, or his pet kitty, Iggy. When the weather is nice, Brann likes to play disc golf, and he proudly points out that Iowa is one of the world's centers for the sport. Iggy does not play.

—❦ GLOSSARY ❦—

amulet (AM-yoo-luht)—a stone or a charm that protects its wearer against evil

burial ground (BARE-ee-uhl GROWND)—a sacred place used as a cemetary

cannibalism (KAN-uh-buhl-iz-uhm)—the eating of human flesh by a person

elder (EL-dur)—someone who is older; in ancient societies, elders were respected and wise

enchantment (en-CHANT-muhnt)—a magic spell

Mountie (MOWN-tee)—a member of the Royal Canadian Mounted Police, who ride on horses

sacrifice (SAK-ruh-fyss)—to give up something important

sanctuary (SANGK-choo-air-ee)—a special, protected place; sometimes a place where people worship, such as a church, temple, or mosque

wendigo (WEN-duh-go)—an evil supernatural creature in Native American legends

—DISCUSSION QUESTIONS —

1. Throughout the story, Buck and Agate sometimes say, "There is always a better way." Have you ever had a time where you needed to think of a better way to do something?

2. At the end of the story, Buck and Agate decide to quit running from their problems. Were there any times at school or at home when you had to stop running from things and face them head on?

3. Before they start the hunt for their parents, Buck and Agate break into their father's trunk. If they had not done that, how would the story have turned out?